Chasing CHASE LONDON 2: HOMECOMING

Selena

Chasing Chase London

Part Two: Homecoming

Selena

Selena

Chasing Chase London

Part Two: Homecoming

ISBN-13: 978-1-955913-23-2

Acknowledgements

Huge thank you to my patrons who help my books come to life with your generous support, enthusiasm, and kindness: Susan, Valarie, Adriana, Nineette, DesiRae, Amanda, Rowena, Terra, Kandace, Kellie, Emily, Christina, Mindy, Tina, Tran, Alex, Hilary, Jessica, Audriana, Alysia, LRaven, Nikki, Emma, Mrs. A, Amy, Rhiannon, Krista, Crystal P, J, Jennifer, Lena, Jasmine, Megan, Margaret, Jennifer S, Kim, Courtney, Nicole, Nikki T, April, Jennifer S, Tasha, Ashley, Nayomi, Crystal W, Doe, Makayla, Kelly, Rebecca, & Sabrina.

one

Now Playing:
"When I Grow Up"—Garbage

"What about you?" Lindsey asks, turning to me at lunch.

"Me?" I ask, looking up from my sandwich. "What about me?"

Elaine snorts and rolls her eyes. I've been sitting with these girls for a month now, and I've gotten used to their group dynamic. In truth, I find them too intimidating to call true, close friends, but I'm grateful to have a spot at their table and in their lives. I don't say much around them, mostly because Elaine terrifies me a little, and my guilt about crushing on Lindsey's boyfriend festers inside me like a splinter that can't work its way out.

"Yes, you," Lindsey says. "Do you have a dress?"

"You are going to Homecoming, aren't you?" Daria asks. "I mean, obviously you are. Who doesn't go to Homecoming?" She breaks off with a giggle.

Me, that's who. I don't go to Homecoming. I'm almost six feet tall. I don't need heels. And I definitely don't need to dance in them. In general, I'm more aligned with David's opinion when it comes to school dances. They're for people who buy into the social order, not for people who don't even register.

Looking around the table at the cheerleaders, football players, and basketball starters, I realize with a jolt that suddenly I might register. Somehow, overnight, I've become someone. Or at least someone who is visible. More important, I like these someones. No, they haven't replaced Meghan, but I've known her all my life.

I've only know them for a month. These things take time. And effort.

I've been too crippled by my social anxiety to really get to know them and let them know me. And that's on me, not them.

I need to start being braver, to start speaking up, doing things with them. If they're school-only friends, it's because I've chosen not to go to games, preferring quiet evenings with Meghan when she's home from school for the weekend. But lately, she's wanted to stay on campus and do things with her friends more and more. I need to get back on my feet, find some friends, make this happen.

So, if going to Homecoming is what my new friends are doing, I want to go, too. I don't want to be left out, staying home alone one more time while everyone else is out having fun, having experiences, having a life. Maybe school dances are something for people like me, after all. Because my friends aren't just part of the crowd that buys into that sort of thing. They're the crowd that sort of thing was invented for.

"I… I don't have a dress," I mutter to my sandwich. I know they're about to rip into me.

Instead, Daria bounces up and down in her chair and claps her hands. "Yay, shopping!"

"Perfect," Lindsey says. "We'll all go Saturday afternoon."

"Oh," I say, my hope draining away.

"No, no," Daria says. "What's that face for? I don't like face."

"Yeah, it's not pretty," Elaine adds.

I ignore her and turn to Lindsey. "I have to work until six on Saturday."

"Oh," she says, blinking at me as if unable to comprehend what I just said.

"Too bad," Elaine says, looking positively gleeful.

"I'll probably be working on Homecoming night, anyway," I say with a sigh.

"Um, no," Daria says. "Girl, you better ask off work, stat."

"Yeah," Lindsey says. "And we'll go shopping Saturday evening."

"I'm supposed to hang out with Brandon, but I'll just make him come along and hold my purse," Daria says with a sly grin.

Elaine snorts. "That's so pathetic."

"You're just jealous because my boyfriend is whipped, and you don't even know what yours is doing off at school."

"I prefer a man who knows better than to screw around on me, not a little boy who lets me carry his balls in my purse."

"To each their own," Daria says, blowing Elaine a kiss.

After school I'm grabbing my work shirt from my locker when Daria comes by and asks if I want to go to Boehner's Burgers with her and Lindsey. It's like I was only an acquaintance before, but now that I'm dating one of their kind, I've been elevated to official friend status.

Before I go to bed that night, I find Mom working on her laptop at the table. I slip in opposite her, folding my bare legs under me. "So, I'm going shopping with some friends after work on Saturday."

She looks up and pushes the laptop aside. "Really?"

"Oh, and I was thinking I'd go to Homecoming. I guess I should have asked that first. We're shopping for dresses."

She looks like she's about the cry with joy. "Oh, Sky. That's wonderful. Of course you can go."

"I didn't know you were such a fan of Homecoming," I say, crossing my arms in front of me.

"I'm so proud that you're finally going out with some of your friends."

I'm sure she's always wondered what kind of social reject she has for a daughter, what with my lack of slumber parties in middle school and my lack of all parties since. She's probably been getting so desperate she was about to put out a sign advertising free alcohol for minors just to get some people to hang out with me.

Part 2: Homecoming

"I knew that London boy would be a good thing for you, honey. Diana says he's from one of the Faulkner's most prominent families."

"Since when do you care about that stuff?" I ask.

"It doesn't hurt to blend in wherever you live," she says.

There's the Connecticut in her. I knew it couldn't have worn off that quickly.

"So, we're going to blend in by caring about who owns the most car dealerships?" I ask.

"I'm not saying money's the only thing that matters."

"You're not? Then what are you saying?"

Mom sighs. We've always clashed. Dad was our buffer...until he wasn't. Without him, it's easier not to talk to her at all. When I try, the old resentments rise up and spill out my mouth without intention.

"Is that who you're going to the Homecoming dance with?" Mom asks.

"Mom, no. I'm going shopping with his *girlfriend*."

"Oh." She seems at a loss for words. She drags her purse over, opens her wallet, and hands me a hundred-dollar bill. "This for your dress. Oh, I can't wait to see you. You're going to look so beautiful, I just know it."

"Can we afford this?" I ask, staring at the bill in my hands.

"It's not that much, Sky. Take it."

"Wow, thank you so much, Mom." I jump up to give her a quick hug at her unexpected kindness. "I'll text you pictures for final approval before I buy one."

"Just make sure everything's covered," she says.

I roll my eyes. "This place really is rubbing off on you."

"I wanted to talk to you about that," Mom says, a little smile forming on her lips. "It's too early to say for sure, but my final interview at Faulkner Regional went really well."

My heart starts pounding. "Mom, that's...That's great."

"It'll be some long hours the first year or two," she says. "And nothing's official yet. I wasn't going to say anything until the paperwork is signed, but, well, I wanted to tell someone."

"Okay," I say, squeezing myself tighter.

"And, if you wanted to transfer to Willow Heights, I think I could swing tuition," she says, reaching an open hand across the table. "It's only three years until you graduate. It might be a little tight, but it's not too late to apply if you want to transfer."

The thought is startlingly unappealing. I wanted to go there despite Meghan's insistence that it was hell itself. I know private school culture. It was easy to blend in. But now… I'm just starting to make friends. There were a few hiccups, and it's not perfect, but things are starting to go well for the first time since school started. Hell, for the first time in years.

"I think I'm okay," I say, placing a hand in Mom's. "You should save it for a house. And one day, maybe Lily will want to go to Willow Heights."

"That's generous of you."

"Thanks for offering," I say, giving her hand a squeeze. For a second, we sit in silence, and things are okay between us, better than they've been since our bridge washed away.

"Sure, honey," she says. "You know I love you, Sky. I only want what's best for you. If you'll just open up a little, let me in sometimes... Not all the time. Even once in a while..."

I pull my hand away. Just like that, she had to go and push it too far. I can't just open up. I'm not a door. I'm a dam. If I open up, I'll flood the world, hurt the people I care about. I'm not a person who screams into the infinite abyss of the universe. I'm a person who cries into her cupped hands so no one will hear.

"Thanks for the dress money," I say, rising from the table and pushing it back across. "But if it comes with strings attached, I'll use my own."

"No," she says quickly, shoving it at me. "Take it. I want you to have it. No strings. Go shopping with your friends."

"Well, thanks," I say. "If you change your mind, I'll pay you back."

I jog up the stairs and fall into bed, trying not to think about the fact that Dad will miss my first school dance. He won't see me in my dress and get all teary eyed and pretend he's cleaning his glasses. He won't watch me go off to prom, or on my first date. One day, if I get married, he won't be there to walk me down the aisle.

But that's his loss. Not mine.

Ignoring the squeaky springs of the pull-out couch, I roll onto my side and curl up in a ball, hugging my knees to my chest, as if they can block my heart from the pain that lives there like a coal under ashes. Tonight, the ashes were knocked away, and the coal is burning hot and bright enough to steal the breath from me.

In that moment, I forgive Chase. If this is anywhere near how he felt when I stumbled on him that night, I can't hold it against him. Because in this moment, I would do anything, absolutely anything, to make the ache go away. Even if it only lasted for an hour, and it hurt someone else for much longer, I would do it.

Selena

I would carry the guilt of it for the rest of my life if I had to. It would be worth it for those few fleeting moments of relief.

two

Now Playing:
"Self-Esteem"—The Offspring

On Saturday, I meet the girls at the mall to look for Homecoming dresses. Daria finds one right away—she looks like a model in anything. She gets a long yellow dress that fits tightly against her curves. With her brown skin and dark hair, she looks amazing in it. After trying on about ten dresses, I collapse into a leather chair in front of the dressing room.

"Ugh. I'll never find anything. I'm exhausted from looking."

"Sure, you will," Lindsey reassures me. "We'll go somewhere else. You'll find the right one."

"Easy for you to say. You're not freakishly tall and flat-chested."

"You're not freakishly tall," Lindsey says. "You're elegant. I always wanted to be tall."

I've never thought of myself as elegant. I kind of like it. "I always wanted to be short. You're so cute."

"Tall is sexy. Sexy beats cute."

"Short people are petite. I always liked the word petite," I say, feeling a little better.

"I have to get my pants altered by my tailor," she says. "Even 'short' jeans are too long."

"My knees bump the doors in really small bathroom stalls."

Suddenly, we're both laughing. Lindsey is the first person I've met who doesn't make me feel like a complete idiot ninety percent of the time.

And I kissed her boyfriend.

I try not to think about it. I didn't know they were together when it happened. It's his responsibility to tell her, not mine. If it even needs to be told. It will hurt her, and it will never happen again, so maybe she's better off not knowing. It's not like we're carrying on something behind her back. It happened once.

Okay, twice. But once when his mom had just died, and I didn't even know who he was. Plus, I don't even know for sure they were together then. Totally doesn't count.

At the next store, I'm carrying an armload of dresses into the fitting room when Elaine clicks up in her stilettos.

"What's she doing here?" she whispers to Lindsey, but I can hear them from inside the dressing room.

"I invited her," Lindsey whispers back. "Be nice."

"Oh, I see," Elaine says, and I can hear the smirk in her voice. "Keep your friends close and your enemies closer."

I freeze. Shit. Did Chase already tell her?

"She's not my enemy," Lindsey says.

"I'm just saying," Elaine says, her voice catty and smooth, "I'd watch my man around her if I were you."

The hairs on the back of my neck prickle, and I can't breathe.

"Oh, I don't think she's his type."

And there it is. What does it matter if being tall is elegant, or being short is cute? She's his type, and I'm not.

"He's a boy," Elaine says. "Anything with two legs is his type."

"Chase isn't like that," Lindsey insists. "He's different."

"Do you think Chase would ever cheat on you?" Daria asks, not sounding like she really cares. I can hear her nails tapping on her phone, still paying half her attention to whatever app she's using. She doesn't bother to whisper, either. I like that about her. She's catty as fuck, but she doesn't try to hide it.

"Probably," Lindsey says, surprising me with her admission and the nonchalance with which it's

ered. "But I don't think any girl would be stupid
igh to cheat *with* him."

My knees give, and I have to sit down. This is so
d. Do they know what we did? Are they saying all this
where I can hear them to warn me or to threaten me?

"Why's that?" Elaine asks, a tiny sliver of
defiance creeping into her voice.

"It would be social suicide," Lindsey says.
"We're Chase London and Lindsey Darling. Everyone
knows we belong together. Our parents practically
conceived us just for each other."

"Please don't ever say that again," Elaine says in
her blasé tone. "It's so creepy."

"Fine," Lindsey says. "Then, how about this one.
He fills my hole."

"Oh, don't get her started on her whole hole
theory," Daria says with a sigh.

I squirm into a dress and emerge, shaken, from
the fitting room. "What hole-hole theory?" I ask.

Lindsey waves a hand and examines my dress
with a frown. "Oh, it's not really mine. I got the idea

from that movie about the girls who smoke all the tin Anyway, it's basically that women need men by nature because we have a hole that can only be filled by a guy. But guys don't need us, they just want us. It's our job to make guys *think* that they need us, so they don't know that they can live without us while we can't live without them."

"Isn't that a little... I don't know, anti-feminist?"

"Not really," she says, motioning for me to twirl. "Women value relationships more, and men value work and stuff. I read it in a magazine somewhere. It's totally true." Lindsey turns back to the other girls. "If Chase cheated on me, I'd probably take him back. I need him. He fills my hole, like, he completes me. He does things I can't do for myself and takes care of me. But I'd never forgive the girl—I'd have to make sure that Chase thought he needed me and just *wanted* the other girl."

"But he doesn't need you," Elaine says. "He's only with you because he promised his dead mother he'd take care of you."

Part 2: Homecoming

All the air is instantly sucked from the room. Lindsey stares at her friend with wide, hurt eyes, and for a second, I think she'll cry. But then she raises her chin, her lip jutting out stubbornly.

"And if you ever point that out to him, I will end you," she says.

"Whatever," Elaine says, rolling her eyes. "I'm bored of talking about your sham of a relationship. Are we getting a dress or not?"

When I can't find a dress at the mall, Lindsey takes me to this specialty shop where she bought hers. We find two that are nice—a cornflower blue that brings out my eyes, and a dark dusty rose that makes my complexion glow. I end up getting the pink. My mom's hundred covers less than third of it, but I've been working, so I can afford to pay for the rest. The other girls will all look perfect. I can't exactly show up looking like I got my dress off the sale rack at Wal-Mart.

But all evening, I can't stop thinking about Elaine's words and Lindsey's unexpected response. Could it be true?

three

Now Playing:
"Got Me Wrong"—Alice In Chains

When I tell Daria during Lit that I've never been to a football game, she practically falls out of her chair.

"Oh my god, you can't be serious," she shrieks. "Where did you say you're from? Unless you're from the moon or Canada, you should have been to a football game by now."

"I didn't realize it was mandatory for high school students," I say, ducking my head when pretty much everyone in the room turns to stare at us.

"It totally is," she says.

"It wasn't really a big thing in Connecticut." I shrug it off because I don't really want to get into the whole, I used to be invisible issue. I wouldn't call myself popular now, but I'm friends with the popular crowd, which makes me very visible, for better or worse. Thanks to Chase London.

"No offense, but Connecticut sounds really lame," Daria says. "Did you even go to Homecoming?"

"That would be a no."

"You're going to love it so much," she says, bouncing in her seat and making a little silent clapping motion with her hands, since we're supposed to be working on our Beowulf homework. A couple guys gape at her bouncing boobs, but she doesn't seem to notice. "Trust me, football is like, the best thing since sex."

I blush at that, since I know even less about sex than about football. And that's not saying much. "Do you actually like football?" I ask, narrowing my eyes at her. "Like, if you didn't cheer, would you still like it?"

Daria covers her heart, her eyes widening. "You think I'm a football fangirl?"

"Uh...no?" I guess, since she sounds like it's a bad thing. To me, being a fangirl means being super passionate about something like Pearl Jam or Harry Potter. But I'm guessing from the connotation that it means something else here.

She crosses her arms and twists her lips to one side. "You totally do."

"I don't even know what a *football fangirl* is," I admit.

"A girl who pretends to like football because the guys will think she's cool, but really she's just faking the whole 'one of the guys' thing. All she's really after is a good dicking."

"I'm guessing that doesn't describe you."

"My boyfriend plays basketball."

"Okay..."

"Trust me, football is amazing," she says, stroking her hand down her long ponytail. "You'll see. You can't help but get excited. Fall is in the air, the team is winning, the fans get so excited, the lights, the smells… It's magic."

I shrug. "Okay."

Daria drops it, and I don't think about it again until I walk into the cafeteria. As I reach our usual table, everyone stops talking and stares at me. Shit. I must have something on my face. I scan the table for Daria or Elaine, who would both point it out, though for different reasons. I'm relieved to reach my usual spot at Todd's elbow, but before I can sit down, Chase leans back and says, "Hey, virgin."

I almost drop my lunch. My brain goes blank with shock. Did I tell someone that?

Daria grins at me from across the table. "I still cannot *believe* you've never been to a football game."

Football. They're talking about fucking football. Not that it's beyond the realm of possibility that Chase would be talking about something else. He probably knows.

I can still feel the pull of that need aching between my legs, the pinch of his finger pushing inside me the first time, his throaty whisper, "God, you're tight."

I want to hurl my lunch at him. Just when I've started to understand him, he has to go and be a complete and utter asshole.

"Jeez, you'd think she's never heard the word *virgin* before," Elaine says. "Get a grip, Sky."

I slide into my seat, face aflame. Todd nods and gives me a grunt of acknowledgement through a mouthful of burrito.

Chase leans forward so he can see past the five or six people sitting between us. "Daria tells me you're a football virgin," he calls down to me with a wicked smile. "Can I pop your cherry?" He winks at me and then starts laughing with all the other guys.

I consider stealing Todd's burrito and throwing it right in Chase's smug face, but I'm afraid Todd might bite my hand off if I reached in front of his mouth.

"Don't worry, I'll be gentle," Chase calls, still hooting with laughter.

Part 2: Homecoming

"Sorry," I say, hooking my hand around Todd's massive bicep and giving Chase a sugary smile. "I'm not into gentle. I'm going to the game to watch my boyfriend. I hear he can really deliver a pounding." Chase's mouth drops open, and I give him a wink. "On the field, of course."

Chase glares so fiercely I shrink into Todd's side. For a second, no one speaks. Then someone says, "Buuuurn."

All the guys start ooh-ing and punching Chase's shoulders. His eyes stay fixed on me another second, his fury drilling into me until I have to drop his gaze.

"Just ignore them," Lindsey says, patting my leg. "They're all idiots. I think it's awesome that you'll be going to your first Wampus Cats game with me."

"Really?" I ask. "I mean, don't you have to go with the cheerleaders?"

"It's a home game, so we just have to show up a few minutes early. I'll pick you up at seven on Friday."

I nod, relieved that I won't be going alone… And that she took the attention off my lack of football experience. I just wish they'd make fun of me with some other word besides *virgin.*

*

At the game, I sit with a crowd of guys from the basketball team and their girlfriends. The crowd starts cheering before the players even come out, chanting along with the cheerleaders. The stadium isn't big, but it's packed, and the whole crowd stands when the players run out onto the field. Brandon and a few of his friends have painted their faces royal blue and white, and when our team gets ahead early in the second quarter, they all take off their shirts and reveal a lot more than just their faces are painted. I've seen players that rabid on TV, but I didn't think high schoolers were that fanatical.

I have to admit, Daria was right. The mood of the crowd washes over me, and I breathe it in, absorbing it through my pores. The air has a nip of fall, and when the banks of lights blink on, a shiver goes through me, half loneliness and half excitement. I hug myself, bouncing on my toes as the players line up for the snap.

The ball shoots into Chase's hands, and he's moving back, then running sideways, then throwing a long spiral down the field. My breath catches, the collective inhalation of the crowd audible as the receiver races down the field, hands out, eyes up. And then the ball is under his arm, and everyone is screaming at once, stomping the metal bleachers until they shake, pumping their fists in the air as the player slows in the end zone.

Chase shines like a star the whole game. I knew he was the quarterback, and that he was good, but he's better than good. He's amazing. He seems to throw every pass right into the hands of the receivers, and even makes two touchdowns himself—one of which he carries most of the length of the field. As the guys around me yell and hug their girlfriends, I feel that distinct sensation of being out of place again. I'm ecstatic to be part of this world, but I keep wondering, *why*?

Elaine said, "Keep your friends close and your enemies closer," to Lindsey, but a part of me can't help but wonder if that's what Chase is doing. I could ruin him. I could tell Lindsey what happened between us, not once but twice. Why would he put us together, encourage our friendship? Isn't that more dangerous than leaving me invisible, where my word carried no weight? As Todd's girlfriend, I'm not exactly popular, but I'm not no one. And as someone in Chase's circle, it's in the realm of possibility that we'd be alone together. Before, no one would have believed Chase London would look at the likes of me.

Whatever his reasons, I feel a swell of gratitude for the bastard. My life before the last few months seems like a dream. I might as well have not existed for all the notice people took of me at my old school, and for all the things I did. Last year, I was the girl whose dad made the news. I don't have to be that here. Here, I can go shopping with the girls from Faulkner High, go to football games, date a linebacker. A good one too, it appears from his performance at the game.

I watch him a little, but I can't keep my attention from straying to Chase even when he's not on the field.

His snug football pants fit him so well it makes my face warm.

After the game, I trail along with the crowd of basketball players and their girlfriends to the parking lot. A tall black guy with a swagger puts his arm around my shoulders. He stops by our table at lunch sometimes to talk to the guys, and I know he plays basketball, but I can't remember his name.

"You going to the party?" he asks.

Suddenly, I'm overwhelmed by all of it. There are so many people, and I don't know any of them really. But I'm supposed to remember all their names and how they all fit together, to smile and play that I'm not shy and that I belong.

"I don't know," I say. "I hadn't really heard about it."

I look around for a familiar face, someone I know even a little.

"You just did," he says, "My place. Be there." He turns around to point at me with both hands before he jogs off to talk to someone else. I'm not very good at the

29

whole mingling thing. It was better to be in the stands, where everyone was watching the game, and I didn't have to do anything but cheer for our school.

For a few minutes, I stand there alone, trying to decide if I should stay. I'm not brave enough to join a conversation, though they're going on all around me in little groups of people who belong. It's suddenly so obvious that I don't.

The night is cool and damp and windy. I start away from the crowd, only to realize I don't have a ride home. I dread calling Mom, though. I can just feel the questions—why didn't your friend bring you home, are you okay, why are you calling?—and I don't know if I can face her. I just want to be at home by myself, without anyone asking me what's wrong. I want to lie on my bed and cry, and listen to Big Head Todd and the Monsters, and not have to smile or talk or wonder. What was I thinking, imagining I could belong in this crazy loud world of football and lights and gossip and shopping and sex? I don't know anything about any of that.

Part 2: Homecoming

I'm still standing alone, lost in indecision, when the whole crowd starts whooping and yelling. The football players are emerging, dressed in their regular clothes again. Chase has his hands up, and everyone is reaching to slap his hands as he goes by. Suddenly he seems worlds away. I stand and watch from across the parking lot, heavy with the sadness of losing something I never really had.

four

I call Mom's cell phone from a somewhat secluded spot next to the field house. I get her voicemail. Facing all those people, so excited about winning a game when I'm feeling down, isn't very appealing. Plus, I don't want to burden someone with taking me home on the way to the party. I lean against the corrugated metal wall and gather my courage. Todd is my best bet. He's almost sure to agree, and he's a man of few words. He won't pry if I tell him I'm not feeling well. I put on a brave face and head back when I hear cars starting up and roaring off. The last thing I want is to be left here, late at night and miles from home.

When I reach the parking lot, Chase's Maserati comes skidding to a stop beside me, the top down. Half a dozen people are piled inside, hanging over the sides of the car, screaming and hooting. I'm not sure I can deal with Chase tonight, and for once, I don't want to see his smiling, teasing face.

"Your chariot awaits, my fair princess!" Chase yells to me over the raucous celebration.

Before I can protest, Todd's massive arms are around me, lifting me over the side of the car into the pile of bodies inside. Chase slams on the gas, and we go screeching around the parking lot onto the road before I've even settled into Todd's lap. Todd keeps his arms around me and growls into my ear. I laugh involuntarily—he's such a primitive sort of guy, carrying me off in his giant caveman way, growling at me and tickling my ear with his scratchy stubble.

The spirit of victory in the car is contagious, and soon I'm swept up in the celebration, my gloom forgotten. The wind is cold on my face, and Todd's burly arms are warm around me in the chill of the night. I lean back, enjoying the rush of speed and the sounds of happiness and friends all around me. Chase expertly maneuvers the sleek little car around each curve at breakneck speed.

The girls in the car, hair flying wildly, scream at every turn. Awkwardness and self-pity forgotten, I join in. I have no doubt I'll look like an overgrown poodle when we get to the party, but I have to admit, the danger feels exhilarating. I think of my mom, who would have an aneurism if she could see me now, in a car going countless miles over the speed limit, not wearing a seatbelt or even riding in a seat. And I'm glad I didn't go home to her.

When we finally skid to a stop at the top of a hill, everyone piles out, laughing and yelling over the music pouring from the big house. All the lights are on inside, and cars line the street outside.

Part 2: Homecoming

Inside, there's a keg and lots of drinks circling. Someone pushes a beer into my hand, and I silently thank Meghan for her "bad influence" over the summer. At least I'm not a complete amateur.

Once he starts drinking, Todd is loud and boisterous, unlike his usual self. And even though he skips introductions and barely says a word to me, he keeps his arm around me, pulling me along as he talks, slaps hands, and shoulder-hugs fans and friends. It's nice to be by his side, if only to keep from standing around feeling awkward.

Once in a while, he asks if I'm okay, and he tops off my drink every time he gets one. I guess this is what being a football player's girlfriend entails. After a bit of thought, I decide I'm okay with that. I find myself feeling proud to be on his arm, and a little ashamed for it. After two drinks, I'm lightheaded, and I excuse myself to find a restroom. I wait in the hall for a while, leaning on the wall and closing my eyes, letting the pleasant, warm buzz of alcohol run through me. When I finally get to the bathroom, Daria barges in with me.

"You don't mind, do you, sweetie?" she says, slurring a little and pulling the door closed behind us. She pulls up her skirt, sits down, and pees right in front of me. I feel like I've just been initiated by some girl-bonding ritual—no one has ever used the bathroom in front of me except my six-year-old sister.

Daria pulls up her skirt and goes to the mirror to inspect her face while she washes her hands.

"I think I'm drunk," she pronounces before looking at me in the mirror. "Where have you been all night, anyway? Don't you have to pee?"

I reluctantly use the toilet. I've never peed in front of anyone, either, and I'm a little embarrassed. But Daria pays me no mind as she fusses with her hair and pouts into the mirror.

"Do you think my lips are uneven?"

I'm not sure she wants an answer. Her lips are perfect, just like the rest of her. Perfectly groomed and shaped, like someone's ideal of a person instead of a real one. She turns to me, pouting her lips at me while I dry my hands. She stops me as I'm about to open the door, holds me away from her, and then starts smoothing bits of my hair.

"With a little product and a few tweaks, you'd have great hair," she says. She starts searching through the cabinets. Finally she gives up and slams the cabinet shut. "Guys never have anything I need."

She takes my arm and stumbles out of the bathroom, laughing like it's the funniest thing in the world when she trips on her heels and nearly drags me to the floor by catching herself on my shoulder. I catch her arm and stabilize her, and together we wobble our way to the couch.

"Where's my drink? I need a drink," she says.

"No offense, but I seriously don't think you need a drink."

"You know what?" she says. "I'm gonna get another drink. You want one?"

"I think I'm good for now," I say, realizing as I say it that I am. I'm actually happy, and that's something I haven't felt since… Dad. As I'm musing in this hazy state, Daria tries to stand, wobbles on her very high heels, and instructs me to help her up. She makes it on the second attempt and drags me along. In the kitchen, she fills her red plastic cup halfway with southern style whiskey and the other half with diet lemon soda followed by a handful of lemon slices.

"This is the best drink ever," she says, sucking on a lemon. "Taste."

She pushes it to my mouth, and I take a sip of the sweet alcoholic mix. It's way too strong. I look around for someone to help me with Daria. She seems a little out of control, and I'm sure the drink isn't doing her any favors. I'm feeling pretty good, but I've never been drunk like she is, and I've never taken care of someone who's drunk. I'm not sure how it's done. I want to stop her, but I'm not sure how that's done, either. People are milling around, but most of them are strangers or people I've never talked to.

Finally I ask, "Where are Elaine and Lindsey?"

Daria is even more animated when drunk, slurring and waving her drink around. "Who cares about them? They think they're better than us, anyway. Elaine doesn't even drink. You know what, Sky? You're my best friend." She wraps me in a sloppy hug, dribbling her drink down my shirt. I laugh and thank her, noticing with alarm that she's already finished half her drink. I try to take it away, but she pushes it to my mouth again. I take a few more swallows of it, thinking that at least that's more she won't be drinking. I don't want to leave her alone, but I have no idea how to handle her. I look around again, an edge of panic creeping in. I don't even know whose house we're in or how I'm getting home. And where is her boyfriend, anyway?

"Oh my god, the Darlings," Daria shrieks, waving an arm over my shoulder.

I cringe, my ear ringing, and turn to see a trio of built, gorgeous blond guys making their way through the throngs of people.

"Hey, Daria," one of the guys says, staring at her tits with no shame. "Gonna let us run a train on you again tonight?"

"Shut up," she squeals, slapping his broad chest.

Another one of the guys, this one with a swish of golden hair over his forehead, looks me up and down like a popsicle he'd like to lick. "Who's your friend?" he asks.

"This is Sky," she says, looping an arm around the neck of the first guy. "This is Lindsey's brother, Preston. And these are his cousins, Colt and Devlin."

"Never seen you around here before," Colt says, sliding an arm around my waist like it's never occurred to him that a girl might not want him to touch her. Hell, it's probably never happened. He's freaking gorgeous. "You new here, babe?"

"Yeah," I say, wishing I were a little more sober. I look to Daria for help, but she's leaned up against Preston, who has his arm around her and his hand up the back of her skirt.

"Thought so," Colt drawls. "I can smell fresh meat from a mile away."

"Gross."

He laughs and tightens his hold, angling our bodies so we're almost facing. "Where you from, Sky? No, don't tell me. Let me guess."

His blue eyes crinkle at the corners as he smiles, a teasing look that holds just a hint of something vaguely predatory.

"Okay," I say, glancing around in search of a familiar face. This guy comes on way too strong for a novice like me.

"Mmm," he says, leaning in so close his breath skims across my cheek. "Must be Montana. Big Sky State."

"No," I say, swallowing hard. My drunk body is saying something very different from my mind right now, especially when he sways in closer, his hip grazing mine.

"Am I close?" he murmurs against my ear.

"Not even close," I say, torn between letting this stranger seduce me and telling him to fuck off. "Connecticut."

"Well, now you went and ruined all the fun," he whispers into my ear. "I was going to guess again."

"Sorry," I say, my eyes falling closed. Electricity tingles through me at the heat of his breath on my neck.

"That's okay, Montana," he says. "We can make our own fun."

That's when my brain clicks back on. "I have a boyfriend," I blurt, pushing against his solid chest. He doesn't budge.

"Well, I don't see him anywhere," Colt insists, smiling down at me with enough charm to make me forget all about Todd. "How about we go somewhere quiet where we can get to know each other better?"

A hand falls on his shoulder from behind. "She told you she has a boyfriend," Chase says, dragging Colt off me. "Leave her alone."

Colt just laughs and holds up both hands in a lazy gesture of surrender, looking unconcerned by the stormy expression on Chase's face. When Colt's backed off, Chase turns to me. "Stay away from them," he commands, leaving no room for argument.

"What do you care?" I shoot back, suddenly annoyed by his interruption.

"I fucking care," Chase says fiercely, his hand wrapping around mine with painful strength. "Don't you get that?"

"No," I say, yanking my hand away. "I don't get it. You have a girlfriend."

Chase swallows, and the fierceness leaves his eyes, but for once, he remains serious instead of making a joke. My pulse flutters at the intensity of his gaze. "Those guys are Lindsey's family, so they'll be around, and I can't always be here to protect you. So just trust me. They're bad news, and you don't want to get mixed up with them. Okay?"

I cross my arms over my chest and glare. "You don't get to tell me what I want, Chase. You're not my boyfriend. I'm not even sure you're my friend."

"Can you just listen to me for once, and stop being a pain in the ass?" he asks, a crooked smile on his face that sends butterflies spiraling through me. If that other guy could make me tingle, Chase can freaking electrocute me with the amount of electricity crackling between us.

"Fine," I say. "Though if they're Lindsey's family, I'd think you'd like them, considering she's your girlfriend."

"They go to Willow Heights," he says. "They treat Faulkner girls like disposable fuck dolls. And believe it or not, I actually know Lindsey is my girlfriend without you reminding me ten times in every conversation."

"Just making sure," I say, raising an eyebrow.

"You know, you're a real asshole," he says, throwing an arm around my neck and pulling me toward the living room. "Now, let's go find Daria before she passes out and gets gang-banged in the bathtub."

"Wow, I'm so glad I came to this party," I say.

"Never leave your drink unattended," Chase says, pulling me into another room. We find Lindsey filling a cup at the keg, and Chase calls to her. I tense, since he still has an arm slung casually around my neck, but she doesn't bat an eye.

"There you are," she says, sliding over to us and standing on tiptoes to give Chase a quick peck on the cheek. Her fingers close around his forearm, her acrylic nails biting into his golden skin as she stretches up to murmur, "We should make a few rounds, make sure everyone sees us."

I pull away from Chase, acutely aware that people are looking our way, watching curiously to see if Lindsey will freak out that he's got his arm around me. They shouldn't bother. She's too classy to have a fight in the middle of a party.

"On the lookout for one drunk Daria," Chase says. "Last seen being groped by your awesome brother."

"Not again," Lindsey groans, rolling her eyes. "Okay, let's go find them. Then we need to circulate and be seen before you go hide."

"I don't hide," he says. "I just don't care about that stuff. You know that."

"*I* care," she says, giving him a hard look.

Chase sighs. "Okay. But if I'm going to play Ken to your Barbie, I'm going to have to start drinking."

"Here," she says, shoving her red plastic cup into his hand. "Beer has too many calories, anyway."

They go off in search of Daria upstairs while I make a round downstairs. A blonde girl is straddling Colt on the huge couch that runs almost the entire way around the living room, grinding on him like she's got something to prove. Several people are passed out further down the couch, one of them with a full beer between his thighs. Other couples are making out among the various people talking and drinking in other spaces.

After making sure none of the couples include Daria, I go out a side door and find a pool filled with more people—some swimming, some standing, diving, talking, splashing around, holding drinks. They're variously attired from fully clothed to fully unclothed, a lot partially clothed, and a few with bathing suits. I finally see Chase and Lindsey hauling her between them into the house.

Part 2: Homecoming

Daria's drink has me buzzing again, and I'm relieved that she's in good hands. I wander around for a while, for once not awkward. I talk to a few people, dance a bit, and check in with Todd. After a while, I get bored and wander upstairs. There, I spot an open bedroom door, and through it, a small balcony that appears deserted except for patio furniture. Once out there, I find a girl leaning over the railing throwing up. I pat her back for a minute, and then she staggers inside.

I drop into a chair and lean back. The stars are shining coldly in the October night. I can see my breath, but I feel warm inside. The night is filled with the music from below and the noises of so many partygoers laughing and splashing in the pool. It sounds far away, even though I know they're only on the other side of the house. From here, all I can see is a lawn and a long stretch of darkness. Somewhere I can hear a dog barking on and off again. I set my drink on the table and lean forward on my arms and listen to the excitement of the party below.

Suddenly a pair of arms slides around me. I sit up with a start, aware instantly from the hotness of his skin and the electricity in my veins that it's Chase. He steps over the chair and settles behind me, his warm arms around my cold ones. I wonder how long I dozed off. I'm cold and the party noises have dwindled.

"Hey, virgin girl," Chase murmurs, his voice throaty. "Was I gentle enough with you tonight?" His mouth brushes my ear, and I can feel his hot breath tickling the hairs on my neck, can smell the alcohol on his breath. Shivers race through me, and without thinking, I close my eyes and relax back against him, my head on his shoulder, my cheek to his, dizzy with my desire for him and the hammering of my own heart.

A soft sound of pleasure and contentment escapes me. Chase sucks in a breath, and his arms tighten around me, his whole body tensing. He nuzzles into my hair, his hot mouth against my ear, sending shivers of longing through me.

Part 2: Homecoming

"You're the sexiest girl here tonight," he says, his voice low and rough with desire. "I want you so bad, Sky."

He brushes a soft, warm kiss across my ear until I'm trembling. It takes a moment for his last words to soak in. I'm so distracted by his soft lips and warm breath that I can hardly breathe myself. Then images flash rapidly in my mind, like shuffled cards falling together in the deck. The parking lot, feeling a conspicuous outsider, the high of the car ride, Todd's company at the party, Daria's drunken affection, Colt hitting on me, Chase chasing him away, and Lindsey dragging Chase off to make their rounds. Sweet, proper, image-conscious Lindsey.

"Lindsey," I burst out, jumping from Chase's embrace and bumping the table, spilling my drink, now mostly melted ice. "Where's Lindsey?"

Chase looks up at me with such a bewildered expression on his face, like he just woke up from a dream and isn't quite sure where he is. "Lindsey," he says, like he's trying to remember. "Lindsey. She's…uh… Ah, shit." He rubs his hand over his face a couple times before he flops back in the chair.

"Yeah," I say. "Shit is right."

"You," he says, trying to point at me but having a hard time keeping his hand from swaying sideways. "You're going to get me in trouble."

My heart slams in my chest as if beating itself against the bars of its cage, trying to break free, to find its home in him. His nearness is overwhelming, the smell of him still clinging to me from his embrace, taunting me with what I can't have.

"You can't keep doing this," I hiss.

His voice drops so low it's barely audible. "Then how come I can't stop?"

Silence falls over us. I cross my arms over my chest, trying to hold myself together. If this is love, why does it hurt so damn much?

No. No, no, no. It's not fucking love. It's a crush. A harmless yet painful, crushing crush.

"There you are," Lindsey says from the doorway, sounding annoyed and relieved at once. I return to the present with a start, hoping it's too dark for Lindsey to see the guilt written all over me.

Chase sits slumped in the chair, his eyes bleary and miserable.

The huge awkwardness of what just happened crashes down on me, and I want to be anywhere but here, on this porch, with my friend and the boy I'm pretty sure I'm falling in love with.

Lindsey looks from Chase to me and heaves a sigh. "Well? You found her. Now let's go."

"He's drunk," I say to Lindsey, pushing past her and into the house.

"You," Chase slurs.

I pause to look back because apparently, I'm a masochist.

Chase points to the spot where I was just standing, but Lindsey walks in front of him and pulls at his outstretched arm.

"You," he says, a smile entering his voice, his finger now aimed at Lindsey. He tugs at her hand, and she slides into his lap with a giggle. I stand there for a minute, sure I'm going to vomit from the pain of my heart wrenching inside my chest as Lindsey wraps her arms around his neck and kisses him on the same chair where he kissed me only minutes ago. At last, I tear myself away and escape like the coward I am.

five

Now Playing:
"Just a Girl"—No Doubt

"Where have you been?" My mother is standing in the kitchen, hands on hips, when I get home the next day.

"I was at Lindsey's," I say, sounding more casual than I feel. I get the orange juice and pour a glass, hoping Mom can't smell alcohol on me.

"I was worried sick," she says, her knuckles white as she clutches the edge of the counter. "I would have called the police by now if it weren't for your cousin."

"Jeez, Mom, chill. I told you I was staying at Lindsey's last night." I feel bad lying. I've never had to do this before, and it doesn't feel good, but I couldn't exactly go home last night.

"You most certainly did not. You said you were going to the football game with her. You didn't say anything about staying overnight."

"I'm almost *sixteen,* Mom. Don't you think I'm old enough to stay at a friend's house?"

"Of course you are. That's not the point. You know I'm happy you're making friends. But the least you owe me is a phone call, or even a text letting me know you're safe. You know I'd be happy to let you go if you just asked me first."

"I called once," I say, the excuse sounding lame even to my own ears. I'm not very practiced at the art of deception. I don't know how other people get out of these things. But I really did call her, and if she'd answered, I would have gone home with her and skipped that horrible party.

"You didn't even leave a message. How was I to know you were okay?"

"The game ended after eleven," I say. "I wouldn't have made Lindsey take me home that late. Of course I told you I was going home with her afterwards."

"I called you a dozen times," she says, her face tight with anger. "Why didn't you answer?"

How can I tell her that I couldn't hear it over the music cranked to maximum volume and the voices of all my drunk, underage friends?

Before I answer, Mom continues. "That was very irresponsible of you. You're grounded for a week. No after school activities except work."

I'm stunned. I've never been grounded in my life. Of course, I've never done anything that warranted being grounded. I know I deserve it, but all my anger seems to well up at her at once.

"That's not fair. How can you ground me for something I told you about? It's not my fault you're so old you can't remember yesterday morning." I slam my glass down on the counter, sloshing orange juice over the sides. Then I run out of the room and up the stairs. Lily is on my bed, listening to my iPod.

"Get out of my room."

She looks at me in alarm. I hardly ever raise my voice at my sister, and there's enough of an age difference that we don't really fight. I'm ashamed of myself even as I'm doing it, but I'm so mad I can't seem to stop myself. I know it has nothing to do with Lily, or even my mom, but I can't hold it all inside all the time. Sometimes, it spills out in the worst ways.

Lily's eyes fill with tears, and she throws my iPod at me and runs out of the room. "Your music sucks anyway," she yells before slamming her door behind her.

"Stay out of my room," I yell after her. I throw myself across my bed and press my face into the pillow, muffling my angry scream. I want to punch someone, something, but the person I'm most angry at is myself.

It's not Mom's fault. Of course she's going to freak out when I don't come home. And I've never been selfish about my music before, so Lily didn't know I'd be in bitch mode today.

Part 2: Homecoming

I punch my pillow and then wrap it around my face as if it can hold back the rage that threatens to spill out of my mouth, my eyes, my every pore. I want to firebomb this whole fucking town.

Lindsey gets everything—Chase, a house with a real bed that isn't in her uncle's old workout room that smells like sweaty socks, her own car. She's cute, and smart, and everyone in the entire school loves her. Her dad is some big-shot lawyer and when she gets home from a party at 4 a.m., there's a plate of sugar cookies with a brown football drawn in frosting on the top of each one, and a note saying "Congrats on the game, Lins. Have some cookies. Love, Mom," with a little heart before 'mom.'

And to top it all off, she's so sweet and nice, I can't even hate her for it.

What do I get? Fucking grounded, that's what.

*

I expect a lecture in the car when Mom drives me to work, but when she finally speaks, it's worse. "You should apologize to your sister. She was pretty upset."

I wonder if moms take a class on how to make their daughters feel like shit or if it's instinctual.

My money's on instinct.

"Fine," I say to the window.

"Still mad at me, I see," Mom says.

"I called you. It's not my fault that you didn't answer."

"You'll just have to take your punishment as maturely as possible and do better next time," she says.

The worst part is that she doesn't believe me— and that she's right not to.

I manage to hold myself together until we get to the mall, where I stumble in five minutes late. I'm actually looking forward to the monotony of Juice King, but I can't seem to focus on the tasks at hand today. I'm a zombie, since I didn't get nearly enough sleep, and I find myself staring off into space instead of waiting on customers. I keep replaying scenes from before I left the party. After seeing Lindsey climb into Chase's lap like she belonged there, my heart stilled, my chest as hollow as the months after Dad.

I stumbled downstairs, wanting to cry so much I could barely swallow past the lump in my throat. I wandered around the house, looking out on the now-empty pool, where a few discarded piles of clothes lay forgotten like empty fast food wrappers blowing around an abandoned parking lot. The hot tub, uncovered and empty but still bubbling, sent a plume of steam into the cold night. In the kitchen, trash littered every counter and table, as well as the floor around the overflowing trashcans. There was something tragic about the aftermath. Once all the celebrating and partying was over, it made the emptiness so much larger.

A few people were passed out around the house, but everyone left after the last keg had been floated. I found trash bags under the sink and started picking up.

"Sky!" David barks, slamming an empty cup down in front of me. "Strawberry Super Sunrise?"

"Right, yeah." I take the cup and begin filling it.

"What's wrong with you?" David grumbles.

I wish I had an answer for him.

*

After work, Meghan comes to get me, so at least I don't have to face Mom again.

"I hear you went to your first game last night," she says, grinning at me as I buckle into the passenger seat. "From what your mom said, it must have gone well."

"Thanks for covering for me," I say. "As well as you could, anyway."

"I told her you had a good head on your shoulders," she says, reaching over to muss my curls. "I knew my baby cuz wouldn't do anything too stupid."

"You do remember the last party I attended, right?"

"Eh, it could have been worse," she says. "You could have gotten pregnant."

"Ha ha," I say. "You have to actually have sex to get pregnant."

"Exactly," she says, pulling to a stop at a red light. "You were practically a saint. So, how was last night? Are you still a saint?"

"It sucked," I admit. "And if by saint you mean virgin, then yes. I still carry the curse."

"Just don't throw it away to get rid of it," she says.

"Wait, am I dreaming, or are you actually getting sentimental about virginity right now?"

"Um, no," she says, holding up a hand as the car starts forward. "I just think, if I had to do it over, I might not be in such a hurry to dump it on the first guy who would take it. I'd make it more about, you know. Actually enjoying it."

"Is that possible?" I ask, skeptical. "First times suck as a rule, don't they?"

She shrugs. "Probably depends on who you're with. Now, tell me why this party sucked. Did it fall short of the last one—by about four inches?" She wiggles her fingers and grins at me.

"Ugh, shut up," I say, pushing her hand away. "And actually, I have a serious question. Remember when you told me to stay away from the mean girls?"

"Yeah…"

"Did I accidentally join them?"

She laughs and shakes her head. "Nah. The mean girls go around dropping these pink origami notes on girls' desks, and once they do, you're pretty much a social pariah. You're forever branded a slut."

"Why?"

She shrugs. "I don't know. They say they're this secret organization, but everyone knows about them. There's even a webpage called *The Slut Club* with a list of all the people in it."

"Why would anyone join that?" I ask, staring at my cousin.

"I don't think they do," she says. "At least not voluntarily. It goes back to, like, the nineties or something. I hear there's a little black book where all the girls who've ever been in it are written down in invisible ink, from before they had internet or some shit. Who knows how much is a rumor, but it's very much still a thing."

"Why doesn't someone get it shut down?"

"And be a narc? They'd find out and initiate you the next fucking day. I'm telling you, they've got spies. And no one's ever recovered from getting initiated. It lasts the rest of high school. Sucks if you get the 'invite' as a freshman."

"Are they like... A gang or something?"

Meghan pulls into a parking spot on the Dixon campus before answering. "Kinda like a really mean girl gang that obliterates your reputation for life."

"What's the point of this again?"

"Do girls need a reason to tear each other down now?" she asks. "Damn, high school's changed a lot since I went."

"You're a freshman in college," I remind her, rolling my eyes.

She laughs. "Those girls are basically terrorists in short skirts. They exist solely for the purpose of scaring the shit out of every girl in high school. Anyone could be next. Take one too many rides at DickneyLand and you're fucked—in the not-fun way. You never know who's next. But don't freak out. Stay off their radar, and you'll be fine, like I said."

I climb out of the car after Meghan. "Has anyone popular been targeted?"

"Not while I was there," she says. "In a weird way, it's a good shield. It would be hard for anyone to take one of those bitches down. They kind of rule the school. Your crowd's probably the only one not scared of them."

"Great," I say. "If they set their sights on our table, they'll pick me off as the weak one."

"The higher you climb, the further you fall."

"Not helping."

"I'm kidding," she says, throwing an arm around me as we enter her dorm. "If they bother to mess with the populars, they'll go for the one on top of the pyramid."

"Lindsey," I mutter, my heart throbbing painfully at the thought of someone maliciously going after my sweet friend. Lindsey wouldn't survive a fall like that. She's too fragile.

"Nah, her family is pretty much untouchable in this town. Even if the rest of her cousins go to Willow Heights and she's the only Darling at Faulkner High, her friends would have her back," Meghan says. "Between them, and Chase London as her boyfriend, and the kind of money she has… Doubtful. Even the mean girls can't compete with that. They're the girls with bad reputations, but it's not like they're all-powerful. If anything, they're probably scared of your friends."

"That's a relief."

Meghan leads me to her dorm room, where we're spending the night bingeing *Buffy* and gummy worms. I'm surprised Mom made an exception for tonight, since I'm supposedly grounded, but Meghan is nothing if not convincing. I wonder what sob story she told Mom to get her to let me out of house arrest this soon. I probably don't want to know.

"Just think of it this way," she says with a sly grin as we enter her room. "You didn't join the mean girls.

You joined the only group worse than them—the rich bitches."

six

Now Playing:
"Say It Ain't So"—Weezer

I want to be mad at Chase for his disgusting behavior at the party, but I can't. I've accepted that I am pathetically and hideously in love with him, and there's not a damn thing I can do about it. When he walks by me in the hall, and our eyes meet, and he gives me a little smirk and a wink, my heart does a dizzying somersault. I can't help the ridiculous grin spreading across my face, either.

He winked at me, I think, ducking my head to hide my giddy smile. *Chase London winked at me!*

Like I said, pathetic as hell.

But I can't be mad at him for being who he is. Chase London, football god, trusted to carry the team. Doting boyfriend, trusted by Lindsey to do whatever she needs him to do. Motherless son, burdened with grief, and class-clown, always having to make everyone laugh so he can laugh, too. He doesn't need me to complicate things further. If anything, he needs a friend he can talk to, not one crushing on him while scheming like the 'football fangirls' Daria mentioned.

At lunch I squeeze in beside Todd as usual. I'm ready with an excuse if he asks where I disappeared to at the party, but he doesn't. Everyone is talking about some drunk girl who fell in the pool and someone had to drag her out so she didn't drown. By the end of lunch, they've already moved on to other topics. The party is over, no doubt just one of many that this crowd has been to this year alone.

"Have you gotten your shoes for Homecoming?" Lindsey asks me.

Shit. I'm going to use my entire savings on this one dance if I'm not careful.

"Who are you going with?" asks Daria.

Elaine smirks at me with one perfectly arched eyebrow raised. I think she's going to say something nasty about me liking Chase, but she just watches me, her eyes glittering with malicious glee.

I shrug, uncomfortable under Elaine's shark smile. "Todd, I guess."

At least, I assumed we'd go together. Todd never actually asked me, but the dance is next weekend. If it's not Todd, it's nobody.

Everyone around me has stopped talking. Lindsey picks at a grape stem. Daria digs through her purse. Todd has stopped eating.

Shit. Something is definitely wrong.

"What?" I ask.

No one looks at me except Elaine, who leans back with a self-satisfied smirk.

"Actually," she says. "Todd is taking me."

I sit there for a second, too stunned to fully register what she said. I've never even seen them talking to each other. And I'd thought he and I were at least kind of seeing each other. I called him my boyfriend the other day, and no one corrected me.

I look to Daria, then Lindsey. They're both picking at their food. Todd's avoiding my gaze as well.

I'm so fucking done.

I get up and walk out, leaving my lunch untouched on the table. What the hell is wrong with these people? Chase has a girlfriend, but I swear he's hitting on me half the time, and the next minute I think it's all in my head. He's obviously not breaking up with Lindsey in this lifetime, so he must just like to mess with me. And now Todd asked *Elaine* of all people to Homecoming when she has a boyfriend in college, and I thought I was seeing Todd. If this is being popular, I don't want any part of it.

I'm furious with myself for letting my guard down with Todd just because he seemed like a nice guy. I'm furious with him for going to Homecoming with

Elaine, and furious with her for the obvious pleasure it brought her to tell me about it. And I'm pissed with the rest of them because they knew all about this, and no one bothered to tell me.

In the bathroom, I slide down the wall in the furthest stall from the door and sit on the floor. I fight the tears, but they force their way out. How could I think these people are my friends? Of course they aren't. It was probably their idea from the beginning to make me look like the biggest joke. I hope they're getting a good laugh. Considering the way they talk shit about each other behind their backs, I shouldn't be surprised.

I hear someone come in the bathroom, and then Lindsey's timid voice. "Sky?"

I brush the tears away without answering. I tell myself they aren't worth my tears, but I'm not sure I believe me. I like these people. I want them to like me. I want to be one of them, to belong, so bad it hurts.

"Sky, sweetie, let me talk to you," Lindsey says, sounding like my mom when she's done something she feels bad about.

I press the back of my head to the metal stall until it aches, but I won't answer. Not when I'm crying. I won't let her see how much they hurt me. Connecticut girls don't fall apart in public.

"We thought you knew," Lindsey says from outside the bathroom stall.

I realize I'm being totally juvenile, locking myself in a bathroom stall, but I don't care. I want to tell sweet little Lindsey to go to hell. Taking a deep breath, I stand up, open the door, and go wash my hands as if nothing happened.

"Sky, really. We all thought Todd had told you."

Daria bursts in, looks from me to Lindsey, and throws her arms around me. "I'm so sorry, Sky," she says. "We all just assumed that you would know. Everyone knows. Todd always takes Elaine."

"*Why?*" I ask, thinking how horrible Elaine is to everyone. She's not even nice to her friends.

"Because. They're Todd and Elaine," Daria says, as if that explains everything.

"Whatever," I say. "I don't even care."

Part 2: Homecoming

"They were like Chase and Lindsey," Lindsey says. I've never heard someone unironically speak about themselves in the third person, but Lindsey's dead serious.

"We both started dating at the start of freshman year, except they broke up. But it was supposed to be us four, best friends dating best friends, y'know? Like our moms. My mom, Chase's mom, and her mom were sorority sisters in college. Our moms married their college sweethearts, who were all friends. They moved to the same neighborhood, so they could raise their kids together. She's my built-in best friend."

"And Chase is your built-in boyfriend." The words taste bitter as poison on my tongue.

"The difference is, Elaine and Todd are a terrible match." Daria takes over the story where Lindsey left off. "He's so nice, and she's...*Elaine*. She'd eat him alive. When they broke up, though, she just said he wasn't ambitious or smart enough for her."

"But Todd's still totally in love with Elaine," Lindsey says. "He'll always be in love with her. So, every time she needs him, he goes back to her."

It's like they're taking turns, each having her own lines in this little drama. Now it's Daria's line. I turn to her, and she delivers right on cue.

"Her college boyfriend won't go to high school dances and stuff. She says it's beneath him. But Elaine wants to do all the high school stuff, so she has Todd on reserve. See, she doesn't really want him, but she wants him waiting for her, just in case. She always wants him to want her."

"Is that why she hates me?" I ask. It kinda makes sense now. I came in and took her back-up boyfriend. But that doesn't make it better. She's a bitch, and Todd deserves more.

"Oh, sweetie, she doesn't hate you," Lindsey says. "She's just a bit... Abrasive."

"That's putting it nicely."

"She'll be nicer once she gets used to you," Lindsey says. "I couldn't ask for a better friend than she's been to me my whole life."

That's great. But where does it leave me? I shouldn't even be pretending I can fit in with these girls. I can't believe I spent $350 on a dress. How could I be so stupid?

"Come on," Daria says. "We'll find you a date. You're amazing. You're gonna make Todd *wish* he was there with you."

Somehow, I doubt it on all counts. I'll probably just end up working that night or go to Meghan's so I'm not sitting around feeling sorry for myself.

It's not Todd I want wishing he was there with me, anyway.

*

Lindsey insists I have to get shoes to go with my dress, which I don't even need, since I won't be wearing the dress. But she's relentless. I try to pull the 'I'm grounded' card, but she shoots it down.

I try telling her I'm happy wearing sandals or flats—hell, in truth I'd be happy going in a dress and Converse—but she says there's no way I'm going to Homecoming in anything other than heels.

She has this power over me, and it's like I'd do anything to earn her approval. I turn into this weird, desperate version of myself when I'm in her presence, constantly panicking that I'll do or say or think the wrong thing, and it'll all come crashing down. The slightest compliment from her, the smallest reassurance that I've pleased her, makes me melt with relief and simultaneously feel like an even bigger loser.

Whenever I leave after hanging out with her, I feel like I'm coming out of a dream—after dreaming I was someone else.

On my day off, I tell my mom I'm going straight from school to work, though I'm not proud of lying to her again. Still, it's not like I'm out at a gang initiation.

I'm literally going shopping. Only a mother from suburban Connecticut could have a problem with that.

I'm waiting for Lindsey outside the school when Chase's Maserati whips around the side of the building and skids to a stop inches from me.

"Hop in, Cinderella," he says out the window. "I hear milady needs some dancing shoes."

"Don't look so glum," Lindsey adds from the passenger seat. "We're going *shopping*, Sky. This is exciting."

"If you say so," I mutter as I climb into the back seat, feeling like an embarrassingly gangly third wheel. I have to fold myself like a pretzel to wedge into the tiny space of his back seat. Whoever invented legs really should have considered an accordion design.

At least I don't have freakishly large feet to go with my praying mantis stature. When we get to the shoe store, I expect him to crack jokes like usual, or get on his phone while we shop. Instead, he looks around and asks about my dress, actually being halfway tolerable for once.

After looking around, he comes back with a nice pair of strappy heels. Instead of letting a salesperson put them on me, he kneels down in front of the chair and slips one onto my foot, looking up at me with an expression that makes it hard to breathe.

"Sky?" he asks, his voice low, his warm hand lingering on the back of my calf. I can feel the crackle of energy between us, thrumming like something alive from the barest touch of his fingers.

"Yes," I whisper, struggling to speak past the lump in my throat. I have to resist the urge to close my eyes and sigh, or scream, or moan.

It shouldn't feel so good. It's not even a sexy place to be touched. But my whole body is melting, turning to a puddle in the chair.

Slowly, he slides his hand down the back of my calf to my ankle.

"I think we found your magic slipper, Cinderella," he says, smiling up at me and holding my foot in his hands.

Part 2: Homecoming

"Oh, those are perfect," Lindsey says, appearing behind him with an excited little clap that shocks me back to reality like a slap in the face. She looks down over his shoulder, oblivious to the storm of heat raging inside me at her boyfriend's touch.

I'm too flustered to even care at this point. Lindsey's gone out of her way to be nice to me, promising to help me find a dress and shoes and a date. And here I am repaying her kindness by pining after her boyfriend.

I curse my stupid, stubborn heart and vow to do better. Then I snatch the shoes from Chase and march up to the register like a girl on a mission to forget she's in love with her best friend's boyfriend.

The whole shoe-finding process takes less than an hour, so Lindsey invites me to kill time at her house so my mom will believe I worked a whole shift at Juice King.

Chase drops us off at Lindsey's enormous, three-story house and drives off, around the circling road through their neighborhood toward his house.

"Come on," Lindsey says, like I didn't just have to sit there the whole way back dreading the moment when they'd kiss goodbye. They spared me today, which means I only have my own guilt to deal with instead of insane jealousy plus guilt.

When we step into her foyer, I try not to gape at the size of everything—the room itself, the giant decorative vases, the crystal chandelier, the winding staircase that looks like something out of a movie. I knew the girl was rich, but damn. This makes my old house in a subdivision look shabby. I cringe when I think of my room at home, what she'd think of my pull-out couch. For some reason, I'm less embarrassed about what Chase thinks of it than I am what Lindsey would think.

"Hey, Linds," calls a male voice.

"My brother," Lindsey says, grabbing my hand and towing me into the kitchen.

A tall guy with damp blond hair is standing in the kitchen holding his phone as he leans on the counter. Last time I saw him, he was in jeans and polo shirt. Today wearing sweatpants and a shirt with the sleeves torn off, revealing drool-worthy, sweat-glazed arms and shoulders and a few tattoos. Dark patches of sweat are soaking through the shirt, like he just got done working out, and damn, it shows.

"You got company," he drawls, his sharp blue eyes raking over me.

I start blushing just from the way he's examining me—especially when I remember the way he talked to Daria at the party, the nonchalant way he slid his hand up her skirt in public, the concern in Chase's eyes when he warned me about the Darling cousins.

"Leave her alone," Lindsey says, opening the fridge. "Sky's a good girl, not one of your skanks."

"Hm," Preston says, taking a slug from an insulated water bottle that was sitting on the counter beside him. "Too bad. I'd hit that after a few beers."

He wipes his mouth on the back of his hand and goes back to his phone, apparently unimpressed with my appearance.

Lindsey hands me a mini bottle of Diet Coke and gestures for me to follow her upstairs. I spare one more glance at her brother, but he doesn't even look our way when we leave.

Nothing boosts a girl's self-esteem like being objectified and then dismissed by a hot guy, even one you weren't interested in to begin with. Especially one who'd require a few beers just to lower his standards enough to consider you.

But whatever. He's Lindsey's brother. It's not like I'd ever go there anyway.

Like her boyfriend is so much better, whispers a voice in my head. I'm pretty sure it's mine, which means I'm going crazy.

"Being grounded sucks," I say with a sigh, sinking onto her bed when we reach her room.

"I bet," she says.

"Let me guess," I say. "You've never been grounded, either?"

"Oh, no," she says. "My parents let me do anything I want."

"Lucky."

"Not lucky," she says, with a sly smile. "Smart. If you learn to ask the right way, your parents will never refuse."

My parents. Right. She doesn't know.

I don't correct her. I don't want to be the girl without a dad anymore. I want to be someone new. Someone popular, who shares secrets in her best friend's room. But knowing Chase didn't tell her does something funny to my heart.

I pull my legs up under me and smile back at her. "All right, genius. Tell me this parental wisdom that can obviously benefit all of mankind."

"You just have to start small," she says. "Ask for something you know your mom will give you. Once she gets used to saying yes, ask for something bigger. Not too big—you have to work your way up."

"And that's how you get everything you want?"

"Well, not everything," she admits. "But more freedom, higher limit on my Amex, less parental involvement. It works both ways, too. The more your parents say yes, the more you'll expect it, and you'll ask with more confidence. It's all about the confidence. Pretty soon, they won't dream of saying no to you."

They.

There's that word again.

And if we really were best friends, if we really trusted each other, now I'd tell her. But something stops me again. I like the high I get from being with Lindsey. I like the approval in her eyes when I promise to go home and try out her theory on my mom. I don't want to see pity or wariness mixed with her conspiratorial smiles. I don't want her to feel obligated, or sorry for me, or suspicious, or any of the other things people do when they find out. For once in my life, I have a friend, and I won't let anything ruin it. Not even the truth.

seven

Now Playing:
"Lump"—The Presidents of the United States of America

Homecoming is such a big deal down here that the dance is the day after the game, since it takes people so long to prepare. I try to convince Mom that it's a special occasion, and not just any game, so I should be allowed to go. She says that she can't go back on her punishment or I won't respect her. It just seems so unfair—the minute I make some friends, here Mom is keeping me away from them. It's not like I'm hanging out with stoners or juvie jumpers.

In the end, she concedes that I can still go to the dance the next night, but not to the game. I vow revenge. I'd rather go the game, where I actually had fun, than have to go to my first dance alone. I didn't find a date because everyone already had dates by the time I found out I didn't. At this point, I'm not even sure I want to go. Everything has left a bad taste in my mouth lately—being grounded, Lindsey being so nice and making me like her so much that I feel guilty every time I'm around her, knowing her boyfriend kissed me and still hasn't told her.

That night after work, Lindsey texts on the OnlyWords app everyone here uses. I wince when I see her messenger handle.

ChasesDarling: Be ready for a spa day tomorrow!
BlueSky: Can't. Have 2 work until 6.
ChasesDarling: We have to get ready for Homecoming. It takes all day. Me and Elaine made HCC.
BlueSky: HCC?

Part 2: Homecoming

ChasesDarling: Homecoming Court.

BlueSky: Congrats. Hate that I missed it. My mom sucks.

ChasesDarling: Ask your Dad next time. They're always easier.

I stare at my phone. Now would be the time, if I was going to open up to her.

But I can't do it by text.

BlueSky: About the dance...

ChasesDarling: Shut up, ur going.

BlueSky: I don't get a choice in the matter?

ChasesDarling: It's Homecoming, not a choice.

BlueSky: I might get fired.

ChasesDarling: Can't you call in? All the girls get ready together. It's tradition. Spa day! Plz come?

I can't say no to her, especially when she begs. Risking her disapproval or disappointment is just unthinkable. She's including me in her tradition. Calling me one of the girls. What if this is my only chance to prove myself, and she realizes how lame I am and gives up on me?

BlueSky: kk. I'll call in.
ChasesDarling: Coming over with C to discuss date situation. Be there in 5.
BlueSky: Sorry, can't. Still grounded.
ChasesDarling: It's cool, moms love me.

I'm already in my pajamas and the last person on earth I want to see is Chase.

I rush into the bathroom and throw on some lipstick and mascara, tie my wet hair in a ponytail and jump into a pair of jeans and a tank top. I hear Lindsey and my mom talking a minute later. I wait for about five minutes, which feels like eternity. I'm hoping by then Lindsey will have charmed my mom, and she has. When I go down, Mom makes no mention of my grounded status. She's chatting away with Chase and Lindsey like they're her best friends.

Why didn't I get the outgoing gene from her again?

"How was the game?" I ask, stepping into the room.

"We won," Chase says with his movie star smile nearly blinding me. "Too bad you couldn't come."

I give Mom some side eye, but she just smiles. "Sky had to work."

Chase's eyes flicker ever so quickly down my body, and a chill explodes over my skin. Crap. Chill bumps, no bra, bad combination. I cross my arms, trying to hide the evidence.

"I could have two dates," Chase says, winking at me.

"Get over yourself," I say, rolling my eyes.

Mom looks horrified, as if I said that to my grandfather or something.

"Aw, come on, my two favorite ladies, one on each arm," Chase says, undeterred by my comment.

"Leave her alone," Lindsey says, scowling at him.

After a bit, Chase checks his phone, and I wonder if they're going to a party. I feel left out for a second, but then I think of Chase and Lindsey kissing in the chair on the balcony and decide I'm not too upset about missing a party.

"Okay, so…" Chase says, looking at me in this strange way, like he's telling me something he knows I don't want to hear. "Greg and his girlfriend broke up, so she's going with her friends. So, I could see if he wants to go with you."

He doesn't sound very confident about that, which hurts a little. After last week, I know Greg as the guy from the parking lot, the one who invited me to the party. But that's literally all I know about him.

"You knew about that the whole time?" Lindsey asks, glaring at Chase. I bet he'll get in trouble for that one later, and I'm even more okay with missing the party. As much as it sucks seeing them acting all cute, it's even worse when they bicker around me.

"Yeah," Chase says with a huge grin. "I just wanted to see if you could come up with anyone else."

"Ugh, you're so annoying," Lindsey says.

Chase just lounges on my aunt's couch, grinning.

Lindsey gets up and gives me a quick squeeze. "Of course he'll want to go with you, sweetie. You won't get to get a mum this year, but we'll make sure you have one next year."

"And a date," Chase says, smiling at me.

"Oh, a mum," Mom says, laughing. "I remember your father telling me about those."

"What's a mum?" I ask.

"You know," Lindsey says, gesturing to her chest. "A *mum*."

"Um… No?"

"It's like a giant corsage," Chase says. "You don't have those in Connecticut?"

"No," Mom says, laughing. "I'd never heard of it before I met Sky's father."

"We're just going as friends," I say quickly, not wanting Mom to start in about my father. "I don't need a corsage." This is the first time I've heard her speak of him in a nostalgic way, and I'm not sure I like it. Especially not around my friends. She should run it by the family first, test it out in private.

"It's not just a corsage," Lindsey says, rolling her eyes at Chase. "It's like... An expression of your personality. I'll show you mine tomorrow."

I shrug. I feel like the biggest loser, practically begging for a date to a stupid dance I don't even want to go to. Still, the whole idea of Homecoming is so classic, and the FOMO is real. After all these years of missing out, I just *have* to go. And some part of me keeps waiting for the other shoe to drop. Yes, I have a life now. I'm hanging out with popular kids. But how long will it last?

I'm not a cheerleader. I'm nobody. As soon as they realize it, as soon as Chase realizes I'm not going to rat him out, are they going to get tired of their new project and lose interest? This year, this chance, might be the only one I get.

I'm annoyed with Chase though, that I had to go through all that mortifying talk of trying to find someone desperate enough to take me to Homecoming, and all along one of his friends was going solo, too.

He hops up off the couch and shakes Mom's hand. "It's so nice to see you again, Ms. Eden."

I wince, checking to see if Lindsey noticed that he didn't call my mother *Mrs. Eden*, but she's texting someone.

Chase turns to me, and there's this painful moment when I'm sure he's about to hug me, and I'm not sure if I'm quite masochistic enough to want it. His crystal blue eyes search mine, and my heart hammers slow and hard in my chest. Chase swallows. He glances sideways at Lindsey, his lips parting as if he's about to speak.

"Well, thanks for coming by," I say. "I guess my dress won't match Greg, but if we're just going as friends, it won't matter, right?"

"Right," Lindsey says, sliding her phone back into her purse and sliding a possessive hand around Chase's arm.

Selena

Chase frowns, his gaze lingering on me a moment longer, and then he follows Lindsey out like the loyal little puppy I know he's not.

eight

Now Playing:
"Celebrity Skin"—Hole

On Saturday, I go to the mall as planned. Mom even lets me have the car, which makes me feel even more guilty for sneaking around. I call Lindsey, and she comes by and finds me hiding out in the car. I can't let anyone from work see me, since I called in sick, so I park far from Juice King's entrance.

"Hurry, we've got a lot to do," Lindsey says as I climb in the back of her yellow Corvette.

"I can't wait," Daria says, clapping her hands and bouncing in her seat. "I love Homecoming. I love all the dances. But Homecoming is the best. Well, and prom, of course. Oh, and Colors Day! And Winter Formal…"

"Of course," I say, rolling my eyes.

"What bug crawled up your ass and died?" Daria asks, twisting around in her seat. "Come on! This is the funnest day ever. A whole day of spa goodness."

"Nothing," I mutter. "I just hate being grounded, and now I have to sneak around."

"Seriously? I wish my mom would ground me so I could sneak out. This is even more exciting. It's like a secret spy mission to get you ready for the dance. Oh my god, I'm so excited!" Both girls are in a state of high energy, fueled by energy drinks as big as Lindsey herself. Daria passes me one covertly, like it's a beer or something.

"Are you allowed to have this? Will your mom ground you for drinking caffeine?" she asks, giving me an exaggerated wink to show she's kidding.

I laugh and shake my head. "Trust me, it's not that thrilling to be on house arrest, but at least caffeine is not off limits."

Daria laughs in her all-out head-thrown-back way.

We go to Lindsey's salon, where her mom and Elaine are chumming it up like old pals, which I guess they are. I realize this is going to be an all-day affair when I see Lindsey take a decorated pink mini-clipboard from her giant handbag.

"Okay, first order of business. Waxing all necessary areas." I don't like the sound of that, and once I'm getting it done, I like it a lot less. I wonder if it's going to be worth the pain I've endured. Nobody is going to be seeing any of my waxed areas, so it's not like it even matters.

A couple hours later, as we're sitting down for pedicures, two more cheerleaders show up to join us. Lucky bitches managed to escape the waxing.

After the pedicures, it's on to facials, massages, and then manicures. Lindsey checks off each necessary procedure on her clipboard. In the afternoon, she goes off to tan with her mom while the rest of us eat from the food court, though Daria has to bring my food to me because I'm afraid someone at Juice King will see me and know I was lying about being sick.

"Lindsey's too nervous to eat," Daria says, digging through her plate of fried rice.

"What's she got to be nervous about?" Jessica asks. "Everyone knows she'll win."

"Win what?" I ask.

Everyone blinks at me in stupefaction.

"*Homecoming queen*," Daria says, like I asked what hairspray was for. I obviously haven't caught on to the important things in life.

"I don't think it's that," Elaine says, sounding bored. "She just wants to look really tiny in her dress. Lindsey never eats when she has to wear a dress. She's afraid her stomach will pooch out."

I can't believe Lindsey could think anything about her was poochy. She's the tiniest person I've ever seen.

"Don't you guys tan, too?" I ask when Elaine goes to throw her trash away.

"Brown people don't go tanning," Daria says. "Lindsey doesn't have a naturally tan bone in her body, and she wants to look perfect tonight. The rest of the girls wouldn't risk burning and being red. Plus, Elaine would never let the sun touch her virgin skin, let alone a tanning bed."

Jessica snorts. "Virgin skin. That's the only thing pure about that girl."

"I don't know," I say. "She might be pure evil."

When the girls laugh, I join them, feeling a bit funny about my first attempt at trashing someone in my new circle, though I can't call Elaine a friend. After the comment, the girls seem to pull me closer, like they've lured me into their malicious gossip and now I'm one of them. Like I only truly belong if I'm willing to cut down one of their own kind. There's something cannibalistic about it. But right then I'm just happy I'm not the one being eaten.

After lunch, Lindsey makes sure everyone has all the accessories we need. "How's your undergarment situation?" she asks me.

"I didn't know I had one." This is all foreign to me—you'd think we were going to a red carpet movie premier by the way we're prepping.

"You can't have a panty line showing," Lindsey says, like I'm missing something totally obvious. "And a thong is out of the question with your dress, because you'd see the strap mark on the side. You have a long, straight dress, so you can't wear underwear."

"Are you serious? I can't freeball Homecoming."

Lindsey looks like I just said the most shockingly obscene thing she's ever heard. She honest to goodness puts her hand over her heart like she might faint.

"What you need is this," she says, pulling out a stack of packages from her bag.

"Pantyhose?" I ask as I unroll them. I hold them up and give Lindsey some serious side-eye. "What the hell is this?"

"It goes from your bra to your knees, shaping and sculpting everything it covers."

"It looks like something my great aunt Mildred would wear."

Lindsey taps her clipboard with her pen. "Chop, chop."

I go in the makeshift dressing room behind a curtain and try it on. Or try to try it on.

"It's too small," I tell her as I squeeze my nonexistent ass into the vacuum seal of spandex.

"It's fine," she calls. "You're so skinny, I'm sure you can fit in my size."

"No, really," I say. "I can't breathe. You're a lot smaller than me. I only look skinny because I'm tall."

She sticks her head in. "That's just how it's supposed to look. See how much smaller your stomach looks?"

I feel like a sausage stuffed into its casing— exposed, with all my imperfections highlighted, not hidden. I reluctantly agree to wear it, though what I need are *more* curves, not less.

"Now," says Lindsey, looking me up and down critically. "About your bra." My bra is pretty nice, and I can't see how she'd have a problem with it.

"Your dress is backless. You can't wear a bra."

My dress is really simple—floor length, backless, dusty rose satin. It's not too low in the front, just a simple gather in the middle that pulls it down a tiny bit to show cleavage, or lack thereof in my case.

"What? No. No way. I tried it on with a bra, and you didn't say anything."

She sighs. "You want to go to Homecoming with your entire bra hanging out?"

"I can't go braless," I say, a bit of panic creeping into my voice. "That would be weird. You'd see…stuff."

Lindsey laughs. "Of course not. I've got these." She hands me a package of pink, jelly-like discs. "They stick right on. No bra needed. And, you get tons of extra cleavage. They're guaranteed to add at least one cup size, but I think it's more like one and a half."

I look them over skeptically. "Are you sure they won't fall out? Because it would be a little awkward if one of my boobs fell off while I was dancing."

She frowns to show me that this is no laughing matter. "They won't fall out. I wear them all the time. Just don't sweat too much. And if you're still worried about it, we can tape them on."

"Um, no, I'm sure they'll be fine." I'm generally not very happy with my flat-chestedness, but I'm not too keen on the idea of stuffing my boobs, either.

After I submit to her undergarment demands, we're whisked in to meet the hairdressers, who primp and prod, straighten, relax, color, wash, comb, curl, blow out, tweak, gel, spray, cut, tease, fluff, dry, twist, roll, cajole, and any other verb that can be done to hair. Two hours later, I emerge from the apron around my shoulders and hardly recognize myself. My hair is razor straight like the other girls usually wear theirs—not a hair out of place, ends even and slanting at an angle. I can't believe that is my hair, long and straight and dark blonde with some lighter highlights.

Selena

Elaine has big, loose hot-roller curls, and Lindsey is getting hers done the same way after some coloring. I've had enough curls to last forever. I love the straightened version. Daria comes bounding up like an overly-excited puppy and prances around showing off her beachy waves. She's the prettiest person I've ever seen in real life, so she's entitled to some vanity. She's as excited about everyone else as herself, and she keeps telling everyone how gorgeous we all look.

Lindsey refuses to be thrown off schedule and marches us out to make-up. "Waxing, check," she says, marking it off her list. "Pedicures, check. Facials, massages, check check. Manicures, tanning, hair, makeup. Check check, check check." I can't believe I'm getting my makeup done by a professional just for a high school dance that I'm going to with some guy I don't even know. But by now, I've surrendered to Lindsey and her determination to make us all look flawless.

After the mall, we go back to Lindsey's to get dressed and ready to go. This is it.

Part 2: Homecoming

After the whole day leading up to it, I'm both exhausted and suddenly exhilarated. I can't help it, after all the build-up. When I look in the mirror at the six of us, I barely recognize myself. We're all lined up in our colorful dresses, smooth and sleek and ruffled and sophisticated. And now I know what it takes to get that airbrushed, polished look of a magazine ad. A whole day of hair removing, stuffing, sucking in, pushing up, straightening, glossing, mixing, matching, painting, starving, coloring and spraying. I look like a different person. A beautiful, flawless person.

I look like one of them.

nine

Now Playing:
"Linger"—The Cranberries

When the doorbell rings, my heart starts beating way too fast. As Chase swaggers in, I realize I was so busy thinking about what I looked like that I wasn't prepared for what *he'd* look like. The sight of him takes my breath. Wearing a tux, he looks even more gorgeous than usual, but also completely at ease, as if it's something he wears every day. He exudes the confidence to look unimaginably irresistible in anything. I'm not sure if it's

Chase or my strangling corset "smoother," as Lindsey called it, but I'm a little lightheaded.

Chase goes straight to Lindsey without a glance at the rest of us, and my heart twists inside me. I know he's with Lindsey and they belong together, like everyone says, but that doesn't stop the painful ache when I see the way he looks at her. He air-kisses both her cheeks.

"You look perfect," he says, smiling at her with eyes that shine for her. I can't take my eyes off them, and yet I can't stand to watch.

Just when I think things cannot possibly get worse, Todd shows up.

He looks awkward enough for himself and Chase both in a tuxedo jacket that strains to contain his hulking form. Elaine gracefully floats over to him and takes his arm. He tries to hug her at the same time, but she pushes him away. An awkward silence falls in the room, and my eyes go back to Chase and Lindsey. They haven't moved. He's still standing in front of her, holding both her hands. If her dress were white instead of blue, they could be saying their vows.

Oh, god. I think I'm going to puke.

They're talking quietly to each other and gazing into each other's eyes, lost in their own little world. My heart stabs with that familiar ache that I've tried so hard to quell, but it just won't go away.

The twelve of us cram into the limousine Chase rented "for his queen," as he put it. I've never seen him so doting and so in love with Lindsey. I thought maybe he didn't love her at all, at least not in the way he should. But now I'm not so sure. He barely acknowledges the rest of us and makes none of his usual jokes and smirks. I don't want to look. I don't want to be here. I want to be far away from him, and her, and the way they're looking at each other.

Like my parents used to look at each other.

Greg distracts me once we're in the limo. He takes advantage of Chase's preoccupation and uses the opportunity to shine. He's funny and outgoing and as relaxed as Chase, but more casual tonight. He keeps his arm around me and generally puts everyone at ease. I look over at Todd, who looks miserable, and Elaine, who looks annoyed, and I'm glad I am not on that date. Although I'm not on the date I want to be on, either—Lindsey is.

At the dance, the DJ plays cheesy rap and catchy pop songs interspersed with a few slow dances. Everyone from our limo immediately melts into the crowd, which is already going strong. Lindsey insisted we not show up early and look too eager. Seeing her and Chase kind of ruined my mood, so I go find a table to sit alone while Greg goes to find his basketball friends.

An hour later, I've downed three cups of punch, and I'm yawning and checking my phone.

"All right, little lady, it's time dance."

I look up to find Greg standing over me, holding out a hand.

"I'm not really a dancer," I admit. "I just came for the free drinks."

"I came to dance," he says. "If you won't dance with me, I'll be force to dance around you. And I don't know if you're ready for that."

"I don't know if you're ready to dance with a girl who's over six feet tall in heels."

"You asked for it," he says, grabbing the back of my chair with one hand and gyrating his pelvis in front of me. It's such an overtly sexual move that my face turns red, though it's mercifully hidden by the darkness. Greg moves in closer, straddling my lap and, sinking lower until he's… well, he's pretty much giving me a lap dance.

"You made your point," I say, laughing and pushing on his chest.

"You going to dance with me or not?"

"Do I have to?"

"That's it," he says. "I didn't want to have to do this, but I'm bringing out the booty."

He turns around and starts shaking his ass at me. By this time, some other people have noticed, and they're all standing there laughing while Greg grinds his ass on my lap.

A prickling heat zaps up the back of my neck like a static shock. When I look up, Chase is staring at me, his blue eyes smoldering with hate.

Well, fuck you, too.

I turn away from him, refusing to let him mess with my head any more tonight.

"Fine," I say, grabbing Greg's hips and pushing him up.

"I know, baby," he says, flicking imaginary dust off his shoulders. "I am fine. Now, let me show you those moves in a vertical position."

If he can act a fool and not care what people think, then I can, too. I'm his date. They'll think I'm clowning around with my goofy date, not being an idiot dancing like a lone stork in a room full of swans. So, without another glance at Chase, I follow my date onto the dance floor, where he proceeds to pull out dance moves that I'm pretty sure didn't exist until tonight.

Looking around at all the grinding, writhing bodies, I realize I'm completely out of my element. Give me a good 90's cover band concert, and I'm jumping around with the best of them, but twerking against a stranger's crotch is not something I know how to do.

Instead, I follow Greg's lead, pulling out the most ridiculous dance moves I can think of, like the running man and the dab. Even though he laughs at me, it doesn't make me self-conscious. I'm not trying to look good, so it doesn't matter that I don't. Pretty soon, I'm laughing at myself right along with him, though laughing makes it distinctly hard to breathe in my corset-like undergarment. After a while, I have to take a break and sit down. When I do, I feel a pulling behind me, and then something gives way.

Panic explodes inside me. Holy shit. Did I just bust the ass out of my dress in the middle of my first Homecoming?

I'll die if I tore a huge hole in my dress and my ass is hanging out.

Before I can faint with humiliation, I discreetly smooth my dress under my butt. It's intact. Thank the baby Jesus.

I didn't rip my dress, but apparently I ripped the seam right out of my 'smoother.' The one that was meant for someone Lindsey's size, not mine. I'm tall and thin, but I'm far from a size 00. It still strangles my waist so tightly I think I might have to cut it off to get out of it. I spot Daria getting drinks, so I hobble over to her and whisper my dilemma. She throws back her head and howls with laughter. When she's done, she sets down her drinks, takes my arm, and marches me to the bathroom.

"Take it off," she says, holding out her hand to me.

I stand there staring at her.

"Well, come on. Hand it over."

"But…I'm not wearing anything under it," I say, heat rising in my face.

"Ah, who cares? Your dress is down to the floor. Even the most epic fall will not get that skirt up far enough for someone to see your ass."

"Great," I say. "Now I'm thinking about all the ways I could trip and fall."

"Just be glad you don't have to walk across the stage," she says. "Now, hurry up, I don't want to miss the show."

In one of the bathroom stalls, I roll down the top of the hideous garment. My lungs expand to full capacity with great relief. "How can you wear these things?" I ask, moaning with pleasure at the feeling of freedom when it's off.

"Are you kidding? I wouldn't wear that if you paid me. They're like medieval torture devices," Daria says from outside the bathroom stall. "You think I'd go to all that trouble for Brandon? I look hot already, and he knows it."

"I'm going to kill Lindsey," I mutter. "She said it wasn't optional."

"You know that whole hole theory of hers?" Daria says. "I think it's a bunch of crap. That's exactly how guys want us to think—that we need them. I'm telling you, they're the ones that need us. I can buy something that gets the job done better than they do, if you know what I mean,"

She winks at me, and I stand there not knowing what to say. Of course I know vibrators exist, but I didn't know people just talked about them out in the open.

She grins and checks the mirror. "As long as I got my toy and my girls, I'm okay. Don't get me wrong, I love me some D. But I sure as hell don't need no man."

"Does that come with a sassy head-roll and some finger snaps?" I ask, depositing the torture device in the trash can. As much as I hated it, I don't really care for the breezy feeling of wearing a dress with nothing under it.

"Damn right," she says, fluffing her hair in the mirror.

"I feel really naked in this," I say, glancing down the front of my body. I've never waxed my lady business before, which makes me even more aware of the cool satin skimming over my most sensitive places.

"Everyone is naked under their clothes," Daria says with a shrug.

We return to the dance, but now I'm paranoid about ripping my dress, so I don't sit down again. I don't want to be forever known as the girl who ripped her dress and ended up naked in the middle of the Homecoming dance. Daria pulls me out onto the floor, and I dance with her and the girls before rejoining Greg. We're cracking up together about my very white-girl take on his smooth moves when I look up and see Chase staring again. This time, he's wearing a strange expression, almost like he's in pain.

He's watching us over Lindsey's head, and of course she's oblivious. I feel sorry for her suddenly—she doesn't have a clue about his 'wandering eye.' It doesn't excuse what I've already let happen, the memory of which eats me up with guilt. At the same time, some sick part of me doesn't want him to stop. Even if I can't have him, it feels good to know. Because when he looks at me like that, the yearning in his eyes makes me ache.

When the next song starts, Chase dips his head to speak to Lindsey. She nods and heads for the tables, leaving Chase standing there amid the grind of bodies.

But he's not looking at them. He's looking at me. For a moment, I believe what's in his eyes, even if he can't say it. That I'm worth risking everything for.

He steps forward, a tentative step, as if to test me. As if to see if I'll turn and run.

But I can't. I'm rooted to the floor. He moves forward again, covering the space between us in a few steps. Reaching out, he takes my hand, his grip sending a jolt of electricity through me. I suck in a breath, swallowing hard as my eyes meet his.

He steps closer, his other hand dropping to my hip. "Dance with me."

Hearing the command in his voice almost melts my resolve before it even starts.

But somehow, I've developed a new courage tonight while goofing around and not caring what anyone thinks. I'm having a great time. Dancing with Chase will just make me torture myself more—with longing for him, and guilt about Lindsey, and confusion about all his conflicting messages.

Selena

"Actually, I'm gonna take a break for a while," I say. I turn around and walk away, a strange sense of elation threatening to lift me right off the floor. I just turned down a guy.

I just turned down Chase Fucking London.

ten

Now Playing:
"You Look So Fine"—Garbage

The thought of what I just did makes me giddy. No one says no to Chase.

He follows me through the crowd, catches my elbow, and walks beside me.

"You look like you're having a good time," he says, grinning at me in a way that melts my resolve to shun him. If he's hurt by the rejection, he doesn't show it. "I saw you pull out some interesting moves over there."

I draw away. "Well, I don't really do this kind of dancing, so I had to improvise," I say, nodding toward the crowd of gyrating bodies. "Plus, the music sucks."

"I know," he says. "But that doesn't mean you can't have fun."

"I was having fun."

"Then come have fun with me," he says, giving me the puppy dog look that does me in every single time. I can see the sparkle of laughter in his eyes despite the sad expression on his face.

"Maybe later," I say, admiring my brilliant refusal. "I really don't like this song."

Chase studies me, his face inscrutable. Before I can figure him out, he turns and disappears into the crowd without another word.

Suddenly, I feel lonely standing there by myself, as if a spotlight has just landed on me. A chill runs up my arms, and I glance around. Yep, people are watching me. People gravitate to Chase, do his bidding. Guys follow him, girls want him. And I just shot him down.

Part 2: Homecoming

I curse myself for brushing him off. I want to dance with him, but I also want him to… To convince me, I guess. To work for it. In my own silly way, I was punishing him for ignoring me all night, and now that I've hurt him back, I wish I hadn't. The plan totally backfired, and I've ended up punishing myself.

I'm standing there conspicuously alone when Daria comes wiggling over and grabs my hand, dragging me back to the dance floor.

"How do you learn to move like that?" I have to yell into her ear over the blaring music.

"It's my Latina blood," she yells back. "The hips don't lie." She shimmies in a circle to show me her belly dancer moves.

"I must have lumberjack blood," I say, laughing.

She keeps twisting and pulling me along. "It's easy. Just shake your ass."

I try, and a minute later, two of the Darling cousins descend and start grinding on us. I try to move away, but Colt keeps pulling me back and trying to get me to hump his leg. Daria is twerking all over Lindsey's brother, so she's no help.

"Are you supposed to be here?" I yell over the music.

Colt pulls me in, grinding his hips against mine. "I'm supposed to be between these thighs, baby," he says. "I bet I could put some rhythm in these hips."

My face burns at the reminder that I'm a clumsy, awkward dork. "I meant, aren't you on our school's rival team? Should you be at our Homecoming?"

"I'm a Darling," he says, an arrogant grin on his face. "Whatever happens in this town, we're there."

"They let rival schools buy tickets?" I ask skeptically.

"Who's going to stop us?" he asks, his smile turning smug as his hands move to my ass and squeeze. "Now, what do you say we take this somewhere a little more private? My car's right outside."

"I better not," I say, struggling to free myself from being groped further. "My friends are all here, and I can't just disappear on them."

"Your loss," he says with a shrug. "A night on my back seat could change your life."

I can only say no so many times. I excuse myself to go to the restroom to escape. On my way I spot Chase, who seems to have none of my reservations about dancing with strangers or leg humping. Guess I didn't hurt his feelings after all.

As I'm leaving the dance floor, Chase appears in front of me. He grabs my hand and pulls me firmly against him with his other arm, as if we're about to tango. I gasp at the sensation of his body pressed up against me with only the silky fabric of my dress and his thin dress shirt between us. When our bodies collide, a buzzing electric charge shimmers through my belly and slips between my legs like a hand.

My lips part in a silent gasp, and I have to fight to keep my eyes from rolling back in my head. The smirk on Chase's smug face is the only thing that stops me.

Even though the Darling boys are every bit as drool-worthy as Chase, they don't make my blood sing like Eric Clapton playing his guitar. Colt rubbed up against me for fifteen minutes and I didn't feel what one moment in Chase's arms makes me feel.

"This one goes out by special request," says the DJ before the music starts pumping again.

Chase grins, leaning in to speak into my ear. "It's the best I could do."

The familiar beat of "This is How We Do It" comes on, and the spell is broken. I can't help but laugh out loud.

"Seriously?" I ask, trying to keep a straight face. "When I said I liked nineties music, this was not what I meant."

"You better believe I'm serious," Chase says, rubbing his chin gently against the side of my neck. "I was gonna dance with you even if I had to carry you out there." Remembering my undergarment situation, I'm infinitely grateful that he didn't try that. Once I think about my lack of adequate coverage, I can't think about anything else.

Instead of grinding against me or pushing his knee between my legs, Chase rests his hands on my hips and moves slowly to the music, letting me keep my feet planted on solid ground. As he moves, I can feel the front of his pants gliding gently back and forth against the silky fabric of my dress, under which I have absolutely nothing but bare, waxed-smooth skin.

My knees go liquid, and I have to hold onto his shoulders to keep myself from melting to a puddle on the floor. If he doesn't stop teasing me, I'm going to get so wet it looks like I had an accident in my dress. But I can't pull away. I can feel the firm muscles of his shoulders under my hands, the strength of his big hands wrapped around my waist, making me feel delicate as a flower. But I don't want delicacy. I want to grind on him hard, to feel the thick throb of him in my palm like I did last summer when I touched him through his jeans. This time, I want it somewhere else. I want to wrap my legs around him and ride his hips.

I've never felt this way about anyone—not even a fraction of this—and it makes me blush at my own lasciviousness. But I can't help myself. He's intoxicating. He's addictive and destructive at once. He's kryptonite that I want to shoot into my veins. He's the poison apple that I want to devour, sucking the juice from every single delicious bite, even knowing that it will kill me.

"You should have worn blue tonight, my blue Sky," he murmurs.

I didn't choose blue because his girlfriend *did* choose it.

Shit, shit, shit.

Chase is looking into my eyes with the exact same look he had right before he kissed me on the couch. I can't let that happen again, especially not in front of the whole school. I'd be executed by Lindsey and her loyalists.

I move a step closer so I can turn my head and not look like I'm avoiding looking at him. In response, he pulls me against him and presses his face into my hair, inhaling deeply. Then he reaches up to my hands, which are still around his neck, and runs his warm hands along my bare arms to my shoulders. He does it again, slowly, and sighs into my hair, sending little shivers all over my body.

I don't know what to do. The sensations in my body are overwhelming me, and I think I'll blow apart, explode in a way a girl from Connecticut is never supposed to do.

Chase's hands move slowly over my shoulders to my shoulder blades. My body is alive with anticipation, each inch of skin waiting for his touch, yearning to come alive the way only he can make me. His hands move with agonizing slowness down my bare back, leaving a tingling of warmth where he's touched me, making me shiver and hold my breath, nearly gasping for more. They stop at the edge of my dress where fabric meets skin. For one moment, I think he's going to put his hands down the back of my dress.

Then each finger fumbles its way over the edge of the hem until just his thumbs are pressing into the bare skin of my lower back. He strokes softly with the rough pads of his thumbs, smoothing them over my lotioned skin. His breath is coming faster, and I pull back a little to see his eyes closed, a little frown of concentration between his brows, and his jaw set in a rigid square.

"Are you okay?" I whisper, hardly daring to breathe. We're barely moving to the raucous party music, an island suspended in the frenzy of bodies. Chase pulls me closer, his hands still on my lower back. He wraps his arms around me, sliding his hands past each other on my back and squeezing me against him, almost lifting me off my feet. His hands find my hips, and he pulls me in, pushing his hips against mine in the same movement.

I'm instantly dizzy, my thighs clenching with need at the sensation of his arousal swollen against mine. A rush of hot excitement sweeps through my body, and I try to step back, but Chase's arms trap me against him. His hands glide over my hips and down the outside of my thighs before raking up, clutching folds of my dress in each hand, his fingers pressing into my thighs so hard it's almost painful. He squeezes my dress in his hands, pulling it so tight that I'm afraid it will rip. For one moment, I want him to.

I want him, all of him. I want every inch of him buried inside me.

Fuck everyone else.

"Come home with me tonight." His voice is throaty and hoarse, a strange, desperate quality to it that startles me. I realize that while I've been lost in the delicious anticipation of feeling his hot hands moving over me, another song has started. I wonder if anyone else has noticed us, or if we just look like any other pair of dancers in the crowd. I wonder where Lindsey is.

"You're with Lindsey," I say, my voice choked with emotion. "What do you want me to say?"

He slowly pulls the handfuls of my dress with one hand and then the other, rocking me against him until I'm so dizzy with need I can hardly stand.

"Say yes."

His words are so simple, as if it really is that easy. It would be. It would be so easy to lose myself to him in body as well as in soul. I know, because I'm already lost. I couldn't stop it if I tried. I've fallen, and there's no going back from the fall.

But loving him doesn't make me a bad person. Going home with him would.

"I can't." I push against his chest. He lets go of my dress and runs his hands back up over my hips and rests them on my waist. After a pause, he lets his eyes travel down my body and then back to my face. The look on his face is open for once—so open it hurts.

"Oh fuck," he says, a small groan escaping as he rubs his hand over his face. His voice is an accusatory knife stabbing into my chest. "What are you doing to me, Sky?"

I feel my face flaming, and I silently curse Daria for making me take off that horrible thing. I'd rather have my breath strangled out of me all night than have anyone know I'm not wearing anything under my silky dress. Especially Chase.

"I'm going to walk away now," I say, trying to preserve what little dignity I have by stepping away from him.

"Then walk away." He says it like a challenge, letting go of my waist with a little shove. I stumble backwards on my heels, and he reaches out and catches my elbow to steady me.

"Chase," I say. "You have a girlfriend. How can I say yes?"

"It's just a label. You make it sound like that matters more than this." He gives me a pleading look and tries to pull me back, but I jerk my arm away.

"It does," I snap. "You have her. There is no *this*."

Our eyes meet, and in that moment, I see that he wants me every bit as much as I want him. But he can't tell me he doesn't have her, and as long as he does, there can be nothing between us. After a beat, he smirks his trademark smirk, and I know whatever glimpse I had of Chase London without the mask of confidence is gone.

"Go on, walk away," he says, the smirk in his voice this time. "I'll just enjoy the view."

"You do that," I say. I toss my silky hair over my shoulder just like one of the girls he likes would do, and I hold my head high as I walk off the dance floor. Let him stare at my ass. Let him enjoy the show. He won't be enjoying any more than that while he has a girlfriend.

To be continued…

Sky's getting in over her head. Can she get over her crush before Lindsey finds out?

Find out in *Part 3: Mid-Season:*
http://books2read.com/ccl3

You can also read all the episodes in Book 3 and more on Kindle Vella!

To keep up with all my releases and get the first chapter of the next episode, join my email group here: https://landing.mailerlite.com/webforms/landing/p9p5n 2